D0969651

For Anna
M.

First American Edition 2005
by Kane/Miller Book Publishers, Inc.
La Jolla, California

© 2003 Albin Michel Jeunesse, 22, rue Huyghens – 75014 Paris
First published in France in 2003 under the title *J'aime...*
by Albin Michel Jeunesse

Library of Congress Control Number: 2004110206

Printed and bound in France by Pollina - n° L93893A

1 2 3 4 5 6 7 8 9 10

ISBN 1-929132-75-1

Minne / Natali Fortier

I LOVE...

Kane/Miller
BOOK PUBLISHERS

I love when
school is out, and Mama
comes to pick me up.

I love to twirl around very fast so my skirt flies out in a big circle.

I love to watch Papa shave and to stick my finger in his shaving cream.

I LOVE to put my feet on top of
Papa's and dance around the room.

When I blow out my birthday candles, I **love** for Mama to relight them so I can blow them out again.

I love when I'm walking with Mama and a grownup she doesn't know says "Hello," to me, and Mama is very surprised and asks, "Who is that? How do you know him? Does he work at your school?"

I LOVE to breathe on a cold window and trace a heart in the mist with my nose.

I love the first days of spring when Mama says, "It's so beautiful today; let's eat outside." And she puts a cover on the table in the garden and we eat radishes and strawberries.

I LOVE the sound of raindrops on my red umbrella.

I LOVE when my brother and I are arguing and he asks me, "Do you want to fight?" And I say, "Okay, but no pinching, no biting and no pulling hair." And then I love when we decide not to fight after all.

I love when Mama measures me and says, "This can't be right. Let's double check. Are you sure you're not standing on your tip toes? Well, then, you must have grown!"

I LOVE when we brush our teeth at the same time and have a spitting contest.

I Love when I stay at my grandparents' house and get to write postcards to Mama and Papa. I write things like, "I slept very late today because we watched a horror movie last night and Grandma forgot to tell me to brush my teeth."

I LOVE to sprinkle cinnamon on
a slice of bread and butter, blow it
off at Sara Gale (whom I don't like),
and then pretend it was an accident.

I love when Papa makes pancakes and pretends to flip them over my head.

I LOVE when I ask Mama's silly friend, "Are you married?" And she answers, "Yes, of course, aren't you?" And I explode with laughter and tell her, "I can't be married, I'm too little." And she says, "Oh. Well, aren't there any little husbands?"

I love it when I want to take Nini, our Irish Setter, to school with me and Mama says, "Oh no, you know very well that Nini has to go to dog school." And I say, "Really? What does she learn in dog school?" And Mama replies in her very serious voice, "Why, how to bark in French, of course. Don't pretend you don't know."

I Love building a fort in the garden with old pieces of wood and rags, and then playing *The Three Little Pigs*.

I LOVE when Grandma shows me photographs of Mama when she was little and says, "It's amazing how much you look alike. Why, she was almost as pretty as you."

I love the smell of my soft, old bunny.
He smells like apples, licorice, soap, roses,
Mama's perfume, soup, rice, toast, wax, wet
dog, and especially, my warm, cozy bed in
the middle of the night.

I LOVE it when we go to Aunt Zaza's and she says, "Today is silly word day. You must use at least one silly word in every sentence. You have to say things like, 'Aunt Zaza poop, may I have a chocolate cookie?' "

When I cross at the crosswalk,
I LOVE to step on just the white lines.

I love when we leave on vacation and Papa has packed all the luggage in the car and I'm in my pajamas because we're going to drive all night. I love when we've said goodbye to the neighbors, locked up the apartment, and are at least 6 miles away and Papa says, "It's good we're leaving in the evening; the drive will be much cooler and more comfortable. We haven't forgotten anything, have we?" And we drive a little farther and suddenly Mama says, "Oh no! I forgot the keys to the house!" And Papa acts like nothing's wrong and drives a little faster and Mama shouts, "Stop!" And then Papa smiles and pulls the keys from his pocket and says, "Fortunately, there is someone in this family who thinks of things." And Mama says, "Oh sweetheart, what would we do without you?"

When I get a cut on my knee and there's a scab, I LOVE to very slowly, very gently, pick it off.

I love Mama's old tee-shirt,
because it smells just like her.

I LOVE it when I ask Mama to read the same story every single night for a week, and then I hide the book and say, "I bet you can't tell me this story by heart," and she never remembers how it starts and then I help her, because I do.

I Love the smell of toast in the morning.

I LOVE to plant seeds and watch
them grow.

I love to walk
around the house in
Mama's high heels.

I love to pick the petals of a daisy and say,
"He loves me; He loves me not; He loves me a
little; He loves me a lot," as I pull each one.
And when I end on "He loves me not," I think
of my neighbor, and when I end on "He loves
me a little," I think of my cousin, and when
I end on "He loves me a lot," I think of a boy
I don't know just yet.

When I'm in the car, I LOVE to read signs and billboards and names of buildings. I love words. I especially love the word *chocolate*.

I LOVE writing my name on the
first page of a brand new notebook.

I **love** it when I say, "There's school tomorrow," and you say, "Maybe we won't be able to go because it's going to snow. Maybe it will snow so much that we won't be able to get the front door open. And maybe we'll have to dig a tunnel through the snow all the way to school. That takes time, you know, digging a tunnel as long as that. Especially when you haven't got a shovel and must dig with your hands and when your hands are freezing because you haven't any gloves." I love it when you say that even though it's practically summer!

I love when we're collecting shells and you say, "I'll be King of the Clams and you'll be Queen of the Scallops."

In the summer, I LOVE to count the hairs on Papa's chest while he's lying on the beach. (I can never count them all.)

I LOVE it when I stand in the water and the tide goes out, and it moves the sand under my feet and swirls around them.

I LOVE the hill behind my grandmother's house, where I can lie in the grass and roll down. One day my brother and I put our arms around each other and rolled down together.

I love my dolls. I have fourteen of them. Sometimes I say to them, "Girls, we're going to the movies," and I line them up in two rows of seven in the guest room (the one with the shutters that close), in front of the bare, white wall. And then we all watch the movie.

I love to try on
Mama's lipstick.

I LOVE to stare at the principal's large, hairy mole.

I love to say to Grandma,
"Tell me a story." Then Grandma,
pretending she doesn't know, says,
"Which story?" "You know! The
Mama story!" "The Mama story?"
"Yes, when she was little and you lost
her in the grocery store, and you were
afraid and ran everywhere looking for
her and you found her by the fruits and
vegetables helping the other
customers. That story."

I Love it when Dr. Suppo taps on my knee with his little hammer, and my leg moves all by itself.

I LOVE to feel the wind against my
hand when our car is going very fast.

I LOVE to write "for Mama," using a different color pencil for each letter.

I LOVE to tuck my hair behind my ears so everyone can see the earrings Aunt Zaza gave me.

I LOVE it when it snows and
we make a snowman with a pipe and
glasses, and toothpicks for hair.
I love making the snowman, and
I love it when you say, "Shouldn't we
make a snowwoman too, so he won't
be lonely?"

I Love it when Mama puts
my hair in two braids and I
look like an Indian princess.

I LOVE keeping a picture of my dog in my desk at school and looking at it sometimes.

I LOVE it when Mama
writes letters and I get to
put on the stamps.

I love it when Margot and I run past the grocer's singing, "The grocer is a gorilla."

I LOVE to look at my stamp collection. I collect bird stamps. One time Mama got a letter with a beautiful pelican stamp and I steamed it off and pasted it in my album.

At the table, when I'm bored, I love to gather up all the breadcrumbs and make little dough balls.

I *love* when my brother's friend comes to the house and kisses everyone except me (he's French), and Mama asks him, "Yvan, why haven't you kissed Clementine?" And then his face turns red.

I love to stand on a chair when dinner is over and announce, "Quiet, please. I will now recite a poem."

After I've had a terrible nightmare, I LOVE when I go into Mama and Papa's room and say, "I want to sleep with you," and they say, "Well, what if we sleep with you, instead?" And they both get in my bed, and then Papa falls out, and then Mama falls out, and we laugh so much because they want to get back in, but I don't need them anymore.

I LOVE to hold a buttercup under my sister's chin and say, "If your chin turns yellow, it means you like butter."

I love to paint my toenails yellow and blue like my babysitter's and to sit down with my legs crossed by balancing on one foot.

I love to have conversations.
I love to sit in the park in front of the
town hall and talk about dinosaurs.
I love your face when I tell you that the
dinosaurs disappeared because they
were asphyxiated by their own farts!
Their own farts! You say in a very
serious voice, "I do not believe it."
"I assure you that it is a fact," I say.
"I will show you where I read it."
And we can't stop laughing.

I Love to count how many people are riding in my car on the subway.

I *love* to trace my ear with my finger,
and then try to draw it.

I LOVE Sunday night when Mama
says, "I don't know what to make for
dinner." And Papa says, "What about
pancakes?" And then we all say,
"What about pancakes?"

I love putting
all my barrettes in
my hair at the same
time: the one with
the butterfly, the one
with the ladybug,
the one with the
ruby and the three
little ones, blue,
yellow and green.

I LOVE to dress up in costumes.

I love to suck on a lollipop while I have gum in my mouth. It's not easy because sometimes they stick together.

I LOVE when I've been sick and I'm almost better and Mama says, "I think I'd better keep you at home one more day, just to be on the safe side."

I love to find a piece of very old chewing gum and chew and chew and chew until it's soft and good for blowing bubbles.